The
HOUND
of
ULSTER

BLOOMSBURY EDUCATION
Bloomsbury Publishing Plc
50 Bedford Square, London, WC1B 3DP, UK
29 Earlsfort Terrace, Dublin 2, Ireland

BLOOMSBURY, BLOOMSBURY EDUCATION and the Diana logo
are trademarks of Bloomsbury Publishing Plc

First published in Great Britain in 2007 by A & C Black, an imprint
of Bloomsbury Publishing Plc
This edition published in Great Britain in 2021 by Bloomsbury Publishing Plc

A catalogue record for this book is available from the British Library

PB: 978-1-4729-8996-3; ePDF: 978-1-4729-8993-2; ePub: 978-1-4729-8995-6

2 4 6 8 10 9 7 5 3 1

Printed and bound by CPI Group (UK) Ltd, Croydon, CR0 4YY

MIX
Paper from
responsible sources
FSC® C020471

To find out more about our authors and books visit www.bloomsbury.com and sign up for our newsletters

The
HOUND
of
ULSTER

Malachy Doyle
Illustrated by Erin Brown

BLOOMSBURY EDUCATION
LONDON OXFORD NEW YORK NEW DELHI SYDNEY

To Louis Isaac Cuchulainn,
he of the bark most tuneful

Contents

Chapter One
Setanta's Dream

Setanta always liked to dream big.

"I'm going to be famous," he boasted to his mother, when he was only six years old. "I'm going to be a Red Branch Knight!"

"Don't be silly, child," said his mother, laughing. "For one thing you're too young, for a second you're too small and for a third we can't afford weapons."

Setanta was sad, then, but his mother put her arm around him. "Only the children of nobles become warriors, love," she told him. "The great king of Ulster, Conor Mac Nessa, would never have one such as you! You'll grow up to be a shepherd, like the rest of our family. Now fetch me some wood for the fire and put such thoughts from your mind."

But Setanta wouldn't give up on his dream. His father often spoke of the band of young people that the king had brought together at Emain Macha, the Red Branch headquarters, to train up as his champions. The young warriors were great hurlers, and specially chosen for their skill at games and sports.

So Setanta made himself a hurley stick from the branch of an ash tree, and found a round stone to use as a ball. As well as the hurley, he made himself a javelin and a spear, a shield and a sword, and he spent every free moment practising, until he was sure that he was just as good as the famous band of young warriors.

Then, one night, when his father was preparing to take their sheep down to the market in Emain Macha, Setanta crept up behind him.

"Could I go with you tomorrow, Father?" he asked.

"It's too far, child," said the man. "You'll get tired, and I'll have to carry you."

"I won't," said Setanta. "I can run for miles."

"It's too busy," said his father. "I'll lose you in the crowd."

"You won't," said Setanta. "I'll stay close by."

"I've too much to do," said his father. "It's hard enough work keeping the sheep together, without having to watch out for a rascal like you."

But Setanta's mother took pity on him. "Oh, let him go with you! He'll have to learn how to drive the sheep one day, so now's as good a time as any."

Setanta ran over and hugged her, for this was the moment he'd been dreaming of.

He hardly got a wink of sleep all night and, by the first light of dawn, when his father came to wake him, he was already up and dressed.

They had a quick bite to eat, gathered the sheep, and set off on their way. It was a long journey, sure enough, but Setanta ran on ahead of the flock, playing at games to shorten the way.

He whacked a stone into the air with his hurley, as high and hard as he could, tossing the stick after it. Running forward, he caught the hurley, held it out and trapped the stone on it. The whole way to Emain Macha, Setanta did this. He never tired and he never dropped the stone, not once.

When they arrived in the town, Setanta saw the king's warriors, every one of them, practising their skills on the green. So, with a whoop and a holler, he ran to join them.

For now was the time to prove that the child of a shepherd was good enough to become a warrior of the mighty king.

Chapter Two
The Young Warriors

Now Conor Mac Nessa, the king of Ulster, was greatly loved by all. He would often go to visit his chiefs and spend time in their houses feasting, which was how he got to know his people, and how they came to love him so well.

There was one person, named Culann, who the king had not got around to visiting yet, but who wished, more than anything, for his lord and leader to eat and sleep in his house. He had no great wealth, for he was a blacksmith by trade, but he had gone to the palace only the day before and begged the king to come and visit.

"I would be pleased to do so," replied the king, much to the blacksmith's delight. "I shall come tomorrow."

On the way to Culann's house the following morning, King Conor stopped by the green to watch his young warriors at play. He was surprised, though, as the ball

rose high into the air, to see an unfamiliar boy, much smaller than the rest, rushing onto the field.

With incredible skill for one so young, Setanta caught the ball on the edge of his stick, dodged round the others, slipped it past them and scored a wonderful goal.

The king was impressed, and wondered who the child was, for he was sure that he had never set eyes on him before.

But his young warriors were not so impressed: the stranger had joined in their game uninvited, and even shown them up in front of their lord and leader.

From then on they used every trick they knew to take the ball away from Setanta and avoid giving him a chance to score.

Setanta, though, was faster than any one of them. He used his size to his advantage, dashing in and out between their legs, collecting the ball and racing with it down the field. Once he'd got the ball, there was no chance of taking it off him, for he'd dart and weave around like he'd been playing all his life. When it came to scoring, Setanta never missed once and, when the young warriors put him in goal to keep him quiet, he stopped every shot.

"Who do you think you are, shepherd's boy?" cried the tallest of the king's warriors, furious with the stranger for having completely shown him up. "You can't just parade on to the field and join in our game without even asking. It is an insult to us and to the king!"

He raised his stick and was about to knock Setanta to the ground, but the smaller boy was too quick for him. He sliced his own hurley low to the grass, chopping the proud fellow's legs out from under him, and it was the leader of the young warriors who ended up on his back.

There were one or two giggles, which made the warrior on the ground even angrier.

"Attack him!" he yelled, and the others began flinging their hurleys at the intruder.

Setanta managed to duck out of the way so that not one of them struck him. They threw their balls at him instead, but Setanta used his arms and his feet to block them and to kick them out of sight.

"I'll sort that shepherd's boy out once and for all!" cried the tallest of the young warriors, running to the side of the field to pick up his spear.

And he might have killed Setanta there and then, but for a great cry splitting the air.

Chapter Three
Big Talk

"HALT!"

Everyone stopped.

"Come here, you," ordered the
king, calling
the unknown
child to his
side. "What
is your name
and how old
are you?"

"My name is Setanta, my lord," answered the child. "I'm nearly seven, and I want to be one of your warriors."

"Where are you from, child?" asked the king. "For I've never seen you round here."

Setanta told him that he lived over the hills, and that he had come with his father to sell sheep in the market.

"You're a bit young to leave home and train to be one of my warriors, Setanta," laughed the king, finding his good humour again. "But you are brave for nearly seven, and if you prove to be as impressive an adult as you are a child, you may well have it in you to become a great warrior. If you will agree to let the others in my school look after you, I will consider allowing you to join."

"I don't need anyone to look after me!" cried Setanta. "I'm stronger and braver than any one of them!"

"Maybe you are," said the king, smiling. "But you are young, and I need to know you will be safe. It is one of my rules that any newcomer must ask the older warriors to look out for them in times of trouble."

"Well, I'll change the rules!" insisted Setanta, scowling at the others. "I'll throw every one of them to the ground until they beg *me* to look after *them*!"

"It wouldn't surprise me if you did," replied the king, delighted at the boy's fierceness, "but I'm afraid I won't be able to watch, for I am on my way to a feast.

Why not leave your fighting until another day and come along with me, for I am most impressed by your strength and courage."

"I'd be honoured, my lord," Setanta answered, "but I can't go until I've challenged these boys and proved that I'm worthy to serve you."

"Fair enough," said the king, chuckling at Setanta's pride. "It is a valiant task for a child of your size, and I wish you luck. I will see you later, Setanta, if you are fit enough to follow after your challenge. I am going with my warriors to the house of Culann the blacksmith.

Do you know where he lives?"

"I don't, my lord," Setanta
said. "But I'll have no trouble
finding you, for as soon as I'm
done here, I'll follow the marks of
your horses' hooves."

King Conor sent word to
Setanta's father, so he would
know where his son was, and then
he and his soldiers rode on to
Culann's house. There, they were
made welcome and a wonderful
banquet was laid out
before them.

As they sat down to eat,
Culann the blacksmith came up
to the king. "Is all your party
present, my lord?" he asked. "Or
are more coming later?"

"They are all here," said
Conor, for his mind was entirely
on the wonderful food and drink
before him on the table. "Why do
you ask?"

"I have a fierce watchdog to guard my land," Culann explained. "It is a savage beast that was brought from Spain and it would take three chains, each held by three people, to hold it down. When I let it loose, no one dares come near, and it will answer to no one but me."

"It is safe to let it off," said the king, with a drink in one hand and a chicken leg in the other. "We are all inside."

So Culann went out, released the hound from its chains, and went back in to the feast. The beast, more like a wolf than a dog, bounded round the walls, barking ferociously to warn off any strangers.

The musicians inside played a little louder so the king was not disturbed by the howling. And, in time, when the creature was convinced there was no one about, it lay down on a grassy mound, where it could keep an eye out for anything that might threaten the safety of its master.

It remained there, with its head on its paws, alert to every movement, every smell and every sound.

Chapter Four
Setanta and the Beast

Setanta set out alone for Culann's house, following the horses' tracks along the road.

The challenge was over and, despite the fact that he was a whole heap smaller than they were, every one of the young

warriors had ended up begging
him for mercy.

To make the journey go more
quickly, Setanta played with
his stone, whacking it up
with the hurley, flinging
the stick after it and
catching them both
as they fell.

When he drew near to Culann's
house, he saw the candlelight
shining from the windows of
the hall and the shadowy outline
of the king and his warriors as
they feasted.

"Soon I'll be joining them," he
said, and his stomach rumbled, for
it had been a long, hard day, with
little to eat.

But the
ferocious
guard dog,
whose ears
were trained
to pick up

the slightest sound, heard him
muttering away to himself, and
let out the sort of howl that would
freeze your blood just to hear it.

Setanta, though, was far too
excited to be put off his stride by
the yowl of a dog. He was looking
forward to feasting with the king,
and telling him how he'd thrown
every last one of his young
warriors to the ground.

"He'll let me join his merry band of young warriors, and I'll be a Red Branch Knight in no time at all!" he muttered happily.

Finding the gate locked, he began climbing over the wall of the enclosure, but the fearsome hound had already spotted him. It licked its lips, gave a low growl, and prepared to pounce.

The moment Setanta hit the ground, he spotted the beast out of the corner of his eye, and couldn't help but gasp at the sight. Stopping dead in his tracks, he fingered his hurley and his stone, for they were the only weapons

he carried, and turned to face the
ferocious creature. The hound
bared its teeth and sprang at him,
its jaws gaping wide.

But with a roar that matched that of the beast, Setanta aimed his stone and flung it deep into the animal's throat. Then, as the creature lay gasping for breath, the boy caught hold of its head and knocked it against a rock.

The musicians stopped playing just as the creature howled its final savage roar. Hearing the sound, a chill ran through the king's heart.

"Alas!" he cried to his warriors. "We should never have come here!"

"Why do you say such a thing, my lord?" asked Culann, shocked and offended.

"That bloodcurdling sound we have just heard," said the king, "has reminded me that I asked a brave young child to follow me to your homestead. All I have done is lead him into the jaws of a wolf! Run outside," he cried, "and see if you can do anything to save the life of that poor innocent child!"

Chapter Five
Cuchulainn

The warriors pulled out their weapons and dashed for the door, but when they got outside, all was silent. Nothing moved in the darkness and they crept around the enclosure, fearful that the hound might come upon them instead.

Then a small voice broke the stillness. "It's all right. I've killed it!"

A guard ran towards the voice and found the dog lying dead on

the ground, and Setanta standing
over its body.

"Thank the stars!" cried the guard, lifting Setanta up onto his shoulders and carrying him back into the hall, where the king sat with his head in his hands.

The guard put Setanta at
the feet of the king and Conor
looked down in astonishment.
Then Setanta told him what
had happened. The assembled
company cheered the boy and the
king hugged and praised him.

But Culann the blacksmith was not so pleased. While everyone else was drinking a toast to the brave Setanta, the owner of the house went out into the yard and wept over the broken body of his dog.

"It's a bad day for my family," he lamented, when he got back inside. "We needed that hound to guard our land and keep us safe, and I will never be able to afford another like it."

"You were right, Conor Mac Nessa," he continued, "I should never have invited you here, for look at the sadness and danger it has brought to me and my family."

The blacksmith turned to Setanta. "Young child," he said, grimly. "You are welcome here for the king's sake, but not your own, for you have taken a good friend from me this day – one who served me well. Without that faithful hound, me and my family will be unable to sleep soundly in our beds."

"I am most sorry, sir, that I had to kill your dog," said Setanta, "but it would have torn me to pieces if I had not! What can I do to help you?"

"How can a child such as you help me?" cried the blacksmith.

"I could guard your house and lands, until you can find another hound to take its place," suggested Setanta.

"I have never heard of a child acting as a guard dog!" cried the king, roaring with laughter. "But if such a thing is possible then I suppose you are the one to do it, for you are the fiercest, bravest child I have ever met. You shall serve our host until I can replace his dog for him."

"There is no beast like it," said the blacksmith, sadly. "It can never be replaced."

"It is through my greed and my forgetfulness that you have lost your protector," said the king. "I shall scour the land, therefore, until I find one of the same breed. I shall have it reared and trained until it is at least as good as the one that died here tonight." "That is a fair price, indeed," said Culann, nodding.

The king turned to Setanta. "To mark your courage and strength, child, from this day forward you shall be called Cuchulainn, the Hound of Culann. You will grow to be a great warrior and, in time, the people of Ireland and Scotland shall hear tell of your deeds and fear shall run through their bones."

Cuchulainn took great pride in the name he had been given, and for many years he carried out his duties, until the dog that the king found and trained was ready to replace the one he had killed.

No raider or wild animal dared go near while Cuchulainn was on guard, for he was as ferocious in his defence of the property as any beast could ever be, and the blacksmith and his family felt safe.

Then Conor Mac Nessa invited
Cuchulainn to come and live in
his palace. The boy joined the
king's young warriors and, in the

fullness of time, became leader of the Red Branch Knights.

He became a great champion of the king, famous through the whole of Ireland for his skill and his fighting. And he was known for the rest of his long and celebrated life as Cuchulainn, the Hound of Ulster.

READING ZONE!

QUIZ TIME

Can you remember the answers to these questions?

- Why does Setanta want to go with his father to the town?

- What is Culann's job?

- What sport is Setanta good at playing?

- Why was Culann sad that Setanta killed the dog?

- What does Setanta offer to do for Culann to make things better?

READING ZONE!

WHAT DO YOU THINK?

Were you surprised by what happened in the story? At the start of the story, did you expect Setanta to become one of the king's warriors? Did you think he would defeat the dog?

READING ZONE!

STORYTELLING TOOLKIT

The author, Malachy Doyle, enjoys
re-writing folk tales like this one.
Do you think it is important for authors
to enjoy what they are writing?

Think about your favourite piece of
writing that you have done. Why is
it your favourite? Why did you enjoy
writing it?

READING ZONE!

GET CREATIVE

Re-read the description of the dog on pages 34–35, then make a list of the words that make the dog sound scary. Can you think of an antonym (opposite word) for each of these words, such as friendly or gentle?

When you have your list of antonyms, use them to write a description of a nice, friendly dog.

Look out for more books in the
BLOOMSBURY READERS SERIES

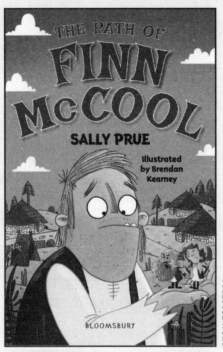

THE PATH OF
FINN McCOOL
SALLY PRUE

Illustrated
by Brendan
Kearney

BLOOMSBURY

9781472967596

Finn McCool is a giant: the biggest giant in the whole of Ireland. However, when he sets out across the sea to Scotland, he realises he isn't the biggest giant in the world. Soon it's up to Finn's wife, Oona to come to the rescue.